I have enjoyed creating and telling stories for many years. The usual recipients of said stories, (poor things!) have been my Wife and children.

These faithful listeners, on hearing each new tale would say, 'You should write it down!'

Finally, I decided I had better take them up on their good advice before my memory fades any further! It is a dream come true to find my work in print, as it is something I have long wished for, but never had the courage to attempt.

I also have a keen interest in art and paint, draw and sculpt whenever I have the time.

THE LONG
JOURNEY HOME

Edward Mark Taylor

The Long
Journey Home

Vanguard Press

VANGUARD PAPERBACK

© Copyright 2003
Edward Mark Taylor

A CIP catalogue record for this title is
available from the British Library
ISBN 1 843860 46 5

*Vanguard Press is an imprint of
Pegasus Elliot MacKenzie Publishers Ltd.*
www.pegasuspublishers.com

First Published in 2003

**Vanguard Press
Sheraton House Castle Park
Cambridge England**

Printed & Bound in Great Britain

Dedication

My wife and Children; for inspiration,
patience and support.

My Mother; for being a 'story-teller' and for her own
special rendition of 'Scrooge'.

The esteemed Mr Dickens; for indelible images.

For Thomas Crimmins, who I never met in this life and
Thomas Brady for memories of youth and music.

God Bless

Edward

Chapter 1

The carriage

A young woman, with sad and haunted eyes, entered the carriage first. She sat down in a corner seat and gazed listlessly through the frosty window. A florid-faced man, in a loud, checked suit followed her, making a great noise settling down. He took from a briefcase, which he then threw carelessly onto the rack above his head, a newspaper folded to the crossword and a pen. He buried his face in this after glancing in the woman's direction and clearing his throat in a most irritating manner.

As the train was pulling away from the station, a man appeared apologetically at the door.

"I beg your pardon," he said addressing the

couple, "All the other carriages are full, do you mind?"

The woman looked in his direction with a weak smile that did not reach her eyes. The florid-faced man cleared his throat, without looking up. The man who entered was tall, thin and very pale, his eyes were watering from the cold and he sniffled into a handkerchief. Sitting down, he removed from his pocket, a train time-table which he began to study avidly. The train gathered momentum and the lights of the city started to slide past at ever increasing speed. It was at this point, that a third man slipped silently into the carriage and sat down.

The three already occupying the carriage seemed almost unaware of his arrival. Where as they pointedly ignored each other, it was as though he wasn't there at all. He was dressed in a dark but light-weight suit, shirt and tie and thin leather shoes. These were completely inadequate for the weather, but he seemed oblivious to this fact. His face was plain and undistinguished and could have belonged to a man of twenty or fifty, it was impossible to say. It was not until he leaned forward, smiled and spoke, that this face was suddenly illuminated.

"Isn't Christmas a wonderful time?" he said, to his three travelling companions. "I think it is the most marvellous time of the year, what do you think?"

The travellers, shocked by this unexpected intrusion into their private thoughts, looked in his direction. If they wondered for a moment how they hadn't noticed him, his smile immediately dispelled this thought. This smile had such a disarming quality, that any witnessing it were immediately enchanted. The apologetic, thin man was the first to answer. Removing from in front of his nose, the handkerchief that had seemed permanently lodged there, he answered somewhat nervously.

"Oh... erm... yes I suppose it is... well for children anyway."

"And we are not children, are we?" the smiling man answered.

The woman gave one of her sad smiles at this but said nothing. The other man cleared his throat and returned to his paper.

"Don't you think," the smiling man continued, "That it is good to act like children, every now and again. To laugh at silly pranks, to make snowmen, to play games and to tell stories. To forget what we are and remember what we were?"

"Nonsense!" the florid man snorted down his nose.

"Nonsense, you say," the man answered, not at all put out by this rudeness. "Why do you say that?"

"It's sentimental rubbish, that's why!" he answered. "It might be fine for children I suppose, they have enough blessed money spent on them! But adults don't have time to enjoy it, they are far too busy!"

"All the more reason, I would have thought," the man smiled. "Everyone needs a little magic in their lives, don't you think?"

At the word magic, a stillness and quiet came over the passengers and a strange atmosphere began to permeate the carriage. It were as though the word, 'magic' was itself Magic. The florid-faced man turned a darker red and a small twitch appeared at the corner of his mouth. It was as if he had just remembered something a bit embarrassing, yet still funny. The woman smiled again, only this time her eyes, which were a beautiful shade of green, lit up as well. The thin man, laughing said,

"I really loved snowball fights! Oh, and Chocolate Selection boxes, they were my favourites!"

As though a flood gate had been opened, the three travellers began to recall things from their past and were soon chatting and laughing amongst themselves. Introductions were made, the thin man was Iain, the woman Anne and the florid man, who at first only gave his surname, was Thomas. Thomas, of the three, was the most reluctant to talk, though he too, had been touched by the strange atmosphere that had fallen on the carriage. They were unmindful of the change that had befallen them and spoke as though they were old friends, not strangers on a train. The smiling man, who had introduced himself as Gabe, was obviously delighted at the outcome of his comments and encouraged his companions to talk freely. After a while he addressed them once again and they gave him their full attention.

"So my friends, you do recall what it is to be a child? Children believe without question. They can experience, accept and believe in things that adults would deny, don't you agree?"

Once again, his words seemed to have a profound effect on them. They gradually fell silent, as though deep in thought. This silence was finally broken by Iain, who started to speak in a quiet voice.

"It is really strange you should say that," he said looking at Gabe, as if he had a question to ask him. "But I've just remembered something that happened to me years ago, I wasn't a child as such, but I was young and still innocent of the world and its pain. It's something I'd completely forgotten about until this moment, but I don't know how I could have!"

"What was it my friend? Why not tell us all about it?"

"It was Christmas… no, I remember now."

The eyes are the windows

"It was Christmas Eve, I had just returned home, after completing the last of my Christmas shopping. My parents were still alive at that time and after saying a quick 'hello' to them, I made myself a hot drink and went to my room.

"I always loved Christmas shopping, especially wrapping the presents. I was well pleased with the paper, labels and ribbon I had bought and placing them on my bed, I unpacked my gifts.

"I had bought my Father a shirt and tie and as I was a little uncertain of his size, I intended to keep the receipt, to be on the safe side! I took, from my overcoat, my wallet, meaning to place the receipt there, and was amazed on opening it, to find three, crisp, new, ten pound notes. I was taken completely by surprise, for I had spent all of my money on the presents and paper I had just brought home. I sat trying to solve the puzzle, then the answer suddenly came to me, Mum and Dad! It was the only explanation. While I was making myself a drink, one of them must have placed the money there, as I had laid my overcoat on the couch next to them when I had arrived home. I had wondered why mum hadn't told me to 'hang it up' as she usually did! Now I had the answer. It was a wonderful surprise, but so typical of them. They knew I would spend all of my money and obviously decided to give me an early Christmas present. I was very touched and immediately went downstairs to thank them. I was not very surprised, when they denied all knowledge of the money. It was again, typical of them, for they loved playing tricks on me and the rest of the family. I thanked them anyway, even though they had very puzzled looks upon their faces and returned to my room. I wish I had known then that it was to be my last Christmas with them.

"After I had finished wrapping my presents, I decided, as it was still reasonably early in the afternoon, that I would return to town. The idea of having the leisure to stroll about enjoying the sights, without the need to shop, but with money to spend if I wished to, was very appealing. I said goodbye to my parents, who were used to me dashing out on the spur of the moment and set off in my car.

"The town centre was bustling, busy and exciting. The shop windows were ablaze with Christmas goods of every description, enticing the unwary to enter. There were also market stalls, selling a bewildering array of items, from the frivolous to the completely useless!

"The lights and decorations were spectacular and I stopped by the huge tree to listen to a choir sing Carols. I must admit, they sang so beautifully, that I, and I think many others, had tears in our eyes. Feeling cold and rather hungry, I visited my favourite café. This was located on the third floor above a busy shop and overlooked the town centre. It was quiet and I sat for a long time, admiring the ever changing scene below.

"Dusk had arrived by the time I left the café but the streets were still alive with movement and noise. Feeling refreshed and not quite ready to go home, I continued to stroll about in a carefree manner. After a short while, I found myself in less populated streets. Many of the shops were already closed, though there were a few, bright with Christmas lights, that were still briskly trading. I turned a corner into an even quieter spot and found myself in front of a dusty, but lighted, window.

"Before me stood a vast array of antique and curious objects. There was a stuffed fox, with miss-matched eyes, a very weather-beaten brass telescope, clocks of every shape and size, many with hands missing. There were swords and spears, gas masks, pottery, figurines, books with faded covers, old toys, oil paintings and lamps and a host of other, less easily identifiable things. I don't know why but I felt compelled to enter the shop, even though it was the kind of place I generally avoided going into. I pushed open the rickety door, which to my amazement opened without a sound and entered.

"Entered, in fact, an 'Aladdin's cave', for the inside was filled, from floor to ceiling, on shelves, stands and the counter, with a multitude of miscellaneous items of every shape, size, age and condition. I was immediately reminded of the shop from 'Alice through the looking-glass', and I half expected a sheep with shawl and glasses to appear at any moment! I nearly jumped out of my skin, when at that moment, a voice spoke from behind me.

May I help you, this voice said, and I turned around to see an elderly man watching me, with an amused look on his face.

"Thin wisps of grey hair stood upright on his head, which was bowed, as though too heavy to be supported by his neck. His hands, that were long and thin, were folded across a pale-yellow waistcoat. He was, in fact, wearing glasses, but the eyes peering over the top of them, were bright and clear.

"Feeling a little self-conscious, I answered him.

'Oh, I was just browsing, I don't really want anything.'

'Don't you?' he said in a very cryptic manner, 'You never can tell.'

'Well you do have some nice things here,' I stammered, feeling a touch embarrassed, 'But I really must be going now.'

"Bidding him all the best of the season I turned hastily to the door and almost collided with a large mirror. Somehow, in all the clutter, I had not seen it before and I steadied it, as it rocked on the shelf it was standing on. It was gilt-framed and would have been completely round, but for two arcs of gilt frame at the top and bottom that made the glass oval in shape. Normally, I would have been self-conscious, standing before my reflection in the presence of a complete stranger, but for some reason I was not. The shape of the mirror had caught my attention and after a moment I realised just what it was that the shape reminded me of. The mirror looked, for all the world, like an eye with upper and lower lids.

'I see you like my 'looking-glass', it is very unusual,' the elderly man said, 'It was originally one of a pair,' and gave a little chuckle at this last remark.

'How much…' I started to say.

'How much do I want for it?' he continued for me. 'Well it is very old and rather unique, wouldn't you say?'

I could only nod my head in answer.

'I couldn't let it go for less than thirty pounds.'

"I know every one has heard the expression, 'my heart skipped a beat' but I am certain at that moment that mine did! Why did he mention that exact sum? The exact amount I had in my wallet and why was I asking in the first place! Hardly aware of what I was doing I told him I would take it. I took from my wallet the three ten pound notes, paid him, left the shop and was half way down the street, before I realised just what I had done. I stopped, in the now deserted, street and cursed myself for a fool. What was I thinking of, wasting all that money on a mirror? It wasn't as though I had my own house to hang it in and even if I did, I wouldn't spend so much on one. The old man had tricked me somehow I thought to myself, and feeling angry at him and embarrassed at my own gullibility, I turned around and headed back to the shop.

"When I arrived, at the shop, I was surprised to find the lights were out, even though I had only just left. I reached for the handle of the door, then for some reason I hesitated. The street seemed unbearably quiet, almost as though it were waiting and watching. The shop itself, looked dreary and depressing and somehow menacing. At that moment,

I began to feel cold and tired and I wanted to go home. Turning my back on the strange shop and feeling that unseen eyes were watching me, I returned to my car. By the time I arrived at my car, I had passed through the brightly-lit and still busy and excited town. This cheered me and helped to dispel the uneasy feelings that had fallen on me. Still very tired, I placed the mirror on the passenger seat and started to drive home.

"I find this next part the hardest to tell, as it is so strange, I can hardly believe it myself. I had decided, because I still felt fatigued, that I would drive home by quieter roads. I was still fairly new to driving and I didn't like to take unnecessary risks. The traffic was heavier than I had anticipated, but I wanted to be home and therefore carried on. I'm uncertain how long I had been driving, as I felt so tired it was as though I were driving on instinct alone. It had started to snow and, distracted by the patterns forming on my windscreen, I didn't see the oncoming headlights, till it was almost too late. My breath caught in my throat, as I twisted the steering wheel hard over. My car swerved and the truck, that narrowly missed me, sped of into the night, leaving the shouts and curses of the driver behind. Ahead of me was a small slip-road and I turned into it and stopped.

I sat, a cold sweat forming on my brow and my stomach churning. I found it difficult to believe, that this day, which I had been enjoying so much, was going so wrong. When I had calmed down slightly, I came to a decision. I would wait until the traffic had eased off, before attempting to carry on my journey. I knew my parents would be worried if I was late, so I decided to look for a telephone. The snow was dying off and leaving my car, I walked back to the junction where the slip road and the main road met. The traffic was still heavy and looking left and right, I couldn't see any sign of a phone. There was, however, a telephone pole on the corner where I was standing. Looking to its top, I could see a single line stretching back down the slip-road and turning back I began to follow it. I walked for about fifty yards, before I came to a break in the hedge that ran along the side of the road. Here I found a gate, it seemed extremely old and rusted at first glance, behind which a long straight driveway led to a house. The telephone wire, had at some point, been fastened to a tall tree, that stood by the gate. From this tree it travelled in the direction of the house. I took this as a lucky sign and pushing open, with some difficulty, the old gate, I walked up the drive.

"Almost from my first step I knew, that the house was unoccupied. I can't say how I knew, I just did. It wasn't just the absence of light or the lack of the sound, this alone might not have convinced me. It was something else, an atmosphere you might say, an atmosphere of desolation and loss. Why I continued in its direction, when I had these feelings, I can not say, I simply did.

"I arrived at a short flight of steps, that led to the front door, I distinctly remember there were five steps and here I stopped. The weather-beaten door was open, held up by one hinge. The windows on either side of it were smashed, and dirty, torn curtains, hung limply there. Through the gap made by the sagging door, I could see directly into the house. Vague shapes, which I assumed were furniture, were lit by thin shafts of pale light. It was a gloomy and saddening sight. Yet for some unknown reason, I was not 'put out' by this vision, nor was I nervous. Instead of turning around and returning to my car, I ascended the short flight of steps without hesitation.

"Inside I saw that the pale light, was emanating from several holes in the roof and ceiling. The floor was a carpet of dust that my feet kicked into little clouds as I moved across the room. There were indeed several items of furniture, a large table, with buckled legs that had a pool of water in its centre, a couch and chairs with springs and stuffing showing and various unidentifiable objects draped in mildewed sheets. The walls were a mass of cracked plaster and peeling paper and there was a damp, unhealthy smell to the place. For all this, I still did not leave, it was as though I knew I had to be there but as yet I did not know why. As I approached the far end of the room, a shaft of light suddenly gleamed on something hanging on the wall. Its shape was familiar and I felt drawn to it. It was at this precise moment that I became aware for the first time that I had the mirror with me.

"How I had carried it without knowing it was there, is a complete mystery to me. I nearly dropped the thing in shock but as my eyes returned to the object on the wall, my fingers clutched convulsively. For there, hanging amidst the muck and mire of years of neglect, was the twin of the mirror I was carrying!

"Carried forward by an unknown force, I stopped immediately before the mirror hanging on the wall. How long I stood, the dark, alien image of myself staring back at me, I do not recall. I could feel my heart beating in my chest and hear the thin gasps of breath whispering past my lips. Eventually, as though my vision were being controlled, I turned my head to the left. On the wall, a short space away, was a pale patch of paper. A pale patch of paper in the form of a oval, with a dull metal hook in its centre.

"At that moment, I knew finally, that somehow I had been chosen, that I was there for a purpose. Almost without a second thought, I moved to my left and placed the mirror back where it was meant to be.

Turning on my heel, I walked to the centre of the room, there, as if once more controlled, I stopped and turned around. A light was now in each mirror, though where it was emanating from, I could not say. As I watched entranced, a movement began in them. At first, a slow swirling mist started to form, which gradually began to take on shape. This shape came slowly into focus, until I was staring, completely engrossed, yet unafraid, at people moving within the mirrors.

"There was a sense of constant motion and I saw countless people come and go, before my wondering eyes. One thing was common to all of this movement, it was all within a Christmas setting. I saw a host of decorations of different size and of every hue, that glittered and danced in a most marvellous way. There were a whole forest of trees, some small and delicate whilst others brushed the ceiling! I saw the dining-table, laden and overflowing with turkeys, ducks, roast and cold, succulent vegetables and piping hot gravy, blazing puddings, mince-pies, shining fruit, steaming bowls of punch and sparkling table-wear. A cornucopia of festive cheer! Over each passing scene a warm and ruddy glow was cast by the high-banked fire and seasonal candles. This was all truly remarkable but more so were the occupants of that room.

"I realised as each happy image passed before me, that I was watching complete lives go by. I saw the innocent face of a babe, turn to the excited face of a child. This became the first flush of bashful youth, which in turn, changed to the wistful face of maturity. Finally a venerable, ancient face, with still smiling eyes, would disappear. This was not sad, as a new face, a new life, would always take its place as the parade of Christmas past and gone continued.

"This cycle moved on and on, whole families and generations passing in the blink of an eye. Each was different, each unique but all bound by that fleeting time, that one season, of peace and fellowship and goodwill.

"Gradually the people before me, began to fade, until the house stood empty and forlorn. Deserted now by the families it had watched over, devoid of its

Christmas cheer, the room failed and fell. I was left with one final image, the duel image of myself, standing in that lonely house. As I watched, for the last time, the image of myself was surrounded by a soft, warm light. A light that seemed to dispel the gloom and neglect. A light that would last, until all turned to dust.

"I realised, again I don't know how, that it was time for me to leave. As I turned away and headed for the door, I noticed, that the light I had seen in the mirrors, was now in fact all around me. At the front door, I paused for one last time and looking back, I bid farewell, silently.

"As I drove home, the spell that had fallen over me, disappeared and I was left with a strange sensation, a mixture of sadness and happiness. As I moved further and further away, the memory of the house, the mirrors, the shop, all gradually faded away. All I was left with was a tremendous feeling of joy. Joy that I was going home. Joy that I was going home to my family."

Chapter 2

The carriage

Iain, with a look on his face that was a mix between wonder and fear, addressed, the still smiling, face of Gabe.

"How could I have forgotten, so magical an event, and how did you know?"

"How I know is not so important," he was answered, "And you didn't really forget, you just had to wait till the right moment to remember."

It was plain that Iain wished to ask more, but before he had an opportunity, Thomas, who was the least affected by Gabe's strange presence, interrupted him.

"Look here!" he said heatedly, "Just who the

devil are you? What is all this nonsense about? Do you take me for a complete fool?"

Gabe answered him.

"No one could call a man, who had built himself a huge and successful business from just a few pounds, a fool."

Thomas's jaw dropped open in shock.

"How did…? Who said…?" he spluttered, at once lost for words.

At that moment a quiet voice spoke from the corner and the three men looked at Anne, who with tears in her eyes said, "I remember."

Snow-flakes

"My Mother had a old-fashioned display case, of which she was immensely proud. Its dark-wood and glass were always highly polished and its contents always free of dust. Its shelves were crammed with an array of ornaments and glass-wear of every shape and size. We children, that is myself, my three sisters and my brother, were never allowed to play in the dining room where the case stood. This case held great fascination for me, with one item in particular being my favourite. This was an immense glass globe, containing a model village covered in snow. It was not the type of snow-scene that you can hold in your hand and shake. In fact, it was as far removed from the modern equivalent as you can imagine. It had a circular base of brass, that must have been at least twelve inches across. I assumed it was heavy, because it was quite an effort for my mother to move it. Despite this fact, she did move it often, usually at my request.

"My brother and my sisters were several years older than I and consequently excluded me from many of their games. This was not too bad in summer when I had my own friends but in winter it meant I spent a great deal of time by myself. Realising this, my mother often allowed me to play in the front room and it was as warm and as cosy a playroom, as any child could want. It was here I played and read and held conversations with my imaginary friends.

"As well as these games, I would spend many an

hour gazing, in rapt attention, at the snow-scene. At its base was a small lever, that when pulled, set the whole model revolving. This action would also set the 'snow' in motion by agitating the liquid inside. The detail of the village inside was truly amazing and obviously the work of a real craftsman. The village was complete with Church, school, shops, homes, hedgerows, gardens, trees, animals and of course people. Each was crafted and painted in remarkable life-like detail and the slow revolution of its motion, added an extra dimension of reality. The interiors of the various buildings could also be seen, through windows and doorways.

"Perhaps its most startling detail was the 'snow' itself, in the way it looked and moved. It fell from the roof of the globe, in slow, steady waves, in what was a remarkable simulation of the real thing. Also on reaching the 'ground' it would cling and lay in the most natural manner. As you can imagine, this beautiful object, kept me mesmerised and filled with wonder.

"That Christmas time, in school, we were making

a frieze for our classroom wall, a part of which was taken up by paper snow-flakes. We had all been amazed, when our teacher had told us, that each individual flake was different, completely unique. She had shown us several slides and we were able to see their complex and intricate shapes. We all had great fun cutting out our snow-flakes, some of which we were allowed to take home. It was a wet and miserable day as I left school and I thought to myself that it should always snow at Christmas. I imagined, as I had many times before, what it would be like to live in a village just like the model one at home. Thinking of the snow scene, I wondered if the 'snow-flakes' it contained were all different. I decided that when I arrived home, I would go and find out.

"My mum was busy, when I arrived home, preparing tea for the family and the extra mouths that my brother and sisters usually brought home with them. I kissed mum and showed her the paper snow-flakes that I had made. Taking a mug of hot chocolate that she had prepared for me, I slipped into the front room where the globe was already waiting on the table. The room was lit only by the light from the coal fire, which crackled and glowed from behind its mesh guard. Leaving the light off, I sat down in front of the globe and pulling the lever, was soon completely engrossed in its magical world. The soft light cast by the fire, gave an extra dimension, an added depth to all I could see. I endeavoured to study individual flakes and although I realised I would do better with the light on, I still left it off. As the fire-light, flickered and danced within the globe, it seemed that the people and animals moved and the buildings had light in them. The heat of the fire, the cosy chair and the slow hypnotic revolution of the globe, all combined to make my eye-lids droop and my head lie heavy on my arms. I must have fallen asleep for a few moments and I awoke with a start to find the globe had stopped revolving. I was just about to set it in motion again, when my eyes were drawn to a building I hadn't noticed before. With my face practically against the glass, I studied the building and I felt my eyes drawn to one particular window. Suddenly there was a loud crack from the fire and a shaft of red light dashed into the globe. A needle thin beam of light that illuminated one building, one window and for a few brief moments of time, the view within that window!

"The shriek that escaped my lips, must have given my Mother a terrible shock, for she dropped and smashed a plate as she came to my aid. She found me sitting on the floor, with a trickle of blood from a bitten lip, dripping onto my dress. Crying inconsolable tears, I mumbled some words about not feeling well. For how could I tell her what I had seen? Wouldn't she think I was lying or playing some macabre new game? For in that brief and shocking moment I saw within the window, an image that shook me to the core.

"Around a bed a family sat, with heads bent, somehow I knew, in sorrow. In the bed a man lay in an attitude of death and holding his hand was a little girl. A little girl with long blond hair, just like mine. A little girl holding the hand of a man who was the image of my Father.

"All that night I wept, it seemed, endless tears,

my temperature raging from burning fever to ice-cold. My Mother put me to bed and eventually I fell into troubled sleep. My first few seconds of waking, were blissfully unknowing, then the nightmare of my experience struck me. I felt as though giant hands had squeeze every last breath from my body and feeling like my heart would break, I wept again, silently.

"I fell asleep once more, but when I reawakened, instead of feeling the same unbearable pain, I felt wonderful. It was as though a huge weight, had been lifted from my chest and an immense feeling of well-being washed over me, I couldn't understand it. The house was very quiet and realising it was still early, I turned on my side, in order to look out of the window. A profound shock awaited me, for there lit softly by pale daylight, stood the globe!

"I could only stare, my whole being was ridged with shock. Afterwards I realised, that my Mother, knowing how fond I was of it, must have placed it there to cheer me up. It was a nice idea but at that moment, the surprise of seeing it dashed over me like iced-water. Unable to stop myself, I moved closer and pulled the lever. The village revolved in its usual way, a clever model and nothing more. Nothing strange or mysterious happened, no visions of impending doom occurred and yet as I watched I felt that the village was also watching and what's more, waiting.

"Not long after, my Mum came into my room and I could tell immediately that she was troubled. I knew that it was more than her concern for me, which was considerable and as she sat down on my bed, I tried to tell her I understood. It was no use, the words just would not come. She was happy at my much improved condition but told me that I must stay home today and that I must be a very good girl. I asked her why, though in my heart I already knew the answer and was therefore not surprised when she told me that my Father was gravely ill.

"I heard these words, as though they were spoken from a great way off, for I had known from the night before that my father was ill. Yet despite this grave news I was happy, for I also knew that he would be well again. I remember squeezing my Mother's hand tightly and telling her, that I knew Dad would be better soon. She had tears in her eyes when she returned my squeeze and agreed with me, and I longed to tell her what I knew but once more I was unable to.

"I spent most of that day in my room playing, distractedly, with my toys, whilst various people came and went. Aunts and Uncles absently patted my head when I saw them and told me I was a good girl. The Doctor visited and I heard him say a move to hospital might be dangerous. I was glad at this, for I felt it was important my Father should stay in his own home. As the long, weary day passed, a feeling of waiting began to grow in me, like some terrible itch I couldn't scratch. I was allowed to see my Father and I sat for a long time holding his hand. Leaning close to his drawn, pale face I whispered in his ear that I loved him and that I knew that everything would turn out right.

"When the rest of the family arrived home that evening, they were almost complete strangers to me. I had never seen them so quiet and subdued, it was awful to see them grieving and I longed to impart that which I knew. Once again the words seemed to catch in my throat, as though something were physically stopping me. Unable to help them and unable to bear the atmosphere, I slipped away to the front room. The room was as warm and cosy as it had been the night before. My Mother, typically, despite everything that was happening, still managed to take care of the family and the home. On the table, lit once again by the fire glow, stood the globe, so innocent and prosaic, waiting I knew, just for me.

"It seems incredible to me now, that I have forgotten for so many years, the events of that night, when I sat in that silent room. Sat staring with rapt attention, at that model village with its fake snow. How could I have forgotten the revolving globe, that had stopped in exactly the same place it had the night before. How could I have forgotten the fire-light, illuminating that room once again. Illuminating that room, where a tiny, figure of a man, who looked like my Father sat up in bed, surrounded by his family and holding the hand of a small girl. A figure of small girl, with long blond hair, who looked just like me."

Chapter 3

The Carriage

A silence fell on the compartment as Anne stopped speaking. Against the window the black night pressed, as the first smattering of snow began to gather on the glass. The train flew across the tracks, as if it to wanted to be out of this night.

As the train swayed and the lights flickered, three pairs of eyes turned in one direction. Thomas, who was the focus of this attention, tried to brazen it out but all the while looking more and more uncomfortable. Finally his nerve gave way, and after muttering a curse, he spoke to his travelling companions in an angry voice.

"Well! What are you all staring at? I know what

you're trying to do, well I think you're all fools!"

Gabe answered him once again, in a gentle voice.

"Just what is it you think we are trying to do? Surely there is no harm in passing the time telling stories?"

"I know you want me to talk about myself!" Thomas practically shouted, "But I will not, I am a very private person, I've made my money by playing my cards close to my chest. Besides, it's all lies, hogwash and nonsense! You are just deluding yourself with sentimentality because of the time of year!"

Iain and Anne, instead of answering this accusation, turned and looked towards Gabe. He smiled at them and they returned it with their own.

"My doubting friend," he spoke kindly once more, "This time of year is special for many reasons. Apart from its blessed and sacred name, it is a time of renewed hope, of charity and generosity. It is also a time when our thoughts turn to those, who are no longer with us, Parents, partners, relatives, good friends, perhaps even... a brother."

At the word brother, Thomas gasped out loud.

His ruddy face drained of colour and his eyes grew wide in shock.

"Br… brother," he stammered, "Why did you say brother?"

Gabe only smiled but it was a smile that said more than words. Thomas looked into his eyes for what seemed an age in that silent compartment, then his shoulders slumped. It were as though a great weight had been lifted from him, his face, his whole demeanour changed. The deep frown that looked permanently etched between his eyes, disappeared. A softer, more youthful look fell over him and when at last he finally spoke, all the loud bluster and arrogance had totally dissipated from his voice.

"I know there is some explanation for all this," his voice softened with emotion. Gabe nodded his head in acknowledgement, "You know all about us, don't you? It doesn't matter, I suppose I will tell you. I have never forgotten, not really, it's just that in the circles I move in there's no place for… for ghosts."

Robert

"My Father died when I was ten years old and it was as though from that moment everything went wrong. We had only just started to recover from the shock of his sudden death, when we learned that all his investments had failed. We were forced to sell our home and my Mother, myself and my sister moved into a small house in the city. For my sister and I, it was very exciting if a little frightening. The city was big and dirty, loud and intimidating and at first we were scared of our immediate neighbours. As time passed though, we realised that they were genuinely good people and they showed us great kindness.

"Money was very 'tight' and Mother was almost at her wits end trying to provide for two growing children. Christmas, before Father died, had always been a time of great joy and though we were never 'spoiled children' it had been for us, a time of plenty. Fortunately, there was a local woman, who ran a Christmas-hamper club and it was to her, my Mother now turned. One of our neighbours had spoken of her honesty and her tolerance to those who had difficulty making regular payments. My Mother started to pay her a small sum of money each week and we were rewarded with a large hamper a week before Christmas day. It was to turn out a very eventful day, for the hamper arrived in the morning and in the evening I was rushed into hospital.

"I had awoken feeling sickly and headachy but a knock at the front door, which had heralded the arrival of the hamper, temporarily improved my condition. My sister and I were thrilled at the prospect of opening the large box and revealing its mysterious contents. Always happy to indulge us, Mother allowed both of us to help. What fun we had, the box was a treasure-trove of excitement. It was packed to the brim with enough tins, packets, boxes and jars to keep us fed till well into the New Year! There were fresh vegetables and fruit, tea and coffee, a huge tin of biscuits and one of mixed savoury crackers.

"Chocolates and sweets were in abundance, a box of soft and spicy mince-pies and a huge succulent ham. There were sauces and preserves, a string bag of unshelled nuts and a box of novelty Christmas crackers. One box, larger than the others, contained a Christmas cake decorated with Santa and sleigh and coated in rock-hard icing! There were many more things besides and each new discovery brought forth exclamations of delight.

"Unpacking the hamper had been immense fun but as the day drew on, my temperature soared and my head ached intolerably. My Mother eventually called the Doctor out, who took one look at me and immediately whisked me off to hospital. When I think of those days, I realise how awful it must have been for my Mother but at the time, I have to admit, my thoughts were strictly for myself. It seemed to me the final stroke of bad luck. I missed my Father very badly, our home and friends were gone and now finally this, it was too much for me and I gave way to self-pity. I must have made a very poor patient and I didn't make things any easier for my Mother when she came to see me. I am certain I left her with the impression that I blamed her for my being ill.

"The ward I was in was decked out cheerfully with a real tree covered in tinsel and twinkling with fairy-lights with a beautiful silver star at the top. Long, brightly-coloured paper streamers, twisted in the air and bunches of balloons were pinned along the walls. The doctors and more especially the nurses, who took care of us, made great efforts to keep up our spirits. I wasn't aware at the time, just how ill some of the other children were but some must have been very ill indeed. I remember one raven-haired girl who was very pale and I thought very beautiful, who was constantly surrounded by relatives and friends. I thought she was some type of star, for she was simply surrounded by flowers and fresh bouquets arrived everyday. One morning I awoke and she was gone, the flowers and visitors had simply disappeared, as though swept away in the night. I asked one nurse about the girl, but she just smiled, plumped my pillows and told me not to worry. Something in her voice, or perhaps her eye, told me a different story and I realised my raven-haired girl would never be going home.

"I slept badly that night and when I did sleep I was troubled by horrible nightmares. One I remember most vividly, was of an empty bed standing before an open doorway. Outside all was totally black and the sheets on the bed were billowing and twisting, as though a huge suction were pulling them towards the open door. I awoke with a scream from this particularly disturbing image and the nurse in attendance had some difficulty calming me down. I drifted in and out of sleep but spent most of the night awake. It was when I awoke from one short spell of sleep, with my sheets twisted about me, that I realised I had a visitor.

"A young boy was sitting by my bedside, smiling at me. After such an awful night, I should have been frightened by this sudden appearance but I wasn't. His smile was so friendly and open, I felt myself respond in the same way.

'Hello,' I whispered, 'Who are you? I haven't seen you before, what are you doing here?'

'I came to talk to you,' he answered in a soft voice, 'Would you like to go for a walk?'

'A walk!' I laughed quietly, feeling very at ease in his company, 'But where to? And what about the nurse?'

'Oh I don't think she'll bother us, come on lets go!'

Unable to resist his friendly persuasion, I slipped out of bed and followed him. We crept silently to the end of the ward, to where the Christmas tree stood.

Its lights gave off a pleasant, low, illumination and my new friend, taking hold of my hand pulled me quickly behind it. I was surprised to find a space behind large enough for us both to sit down. It was marvellous, I felt I had been transported from the reality of the ward, to a magic grotto. The smell of the pine, the shifting shadows caused by the lights and the gleam of the cheerful decorations were wonderful.

'Do you like it?' my new friend asked me.

'Yes, I love it,' I answered, 'But how did you find it? I've never seen you in this ward before.'

'No, I am not from this ward but never mind that now, how would you like to hear a Christmas story?' he asked me with a smile.

In a quiet voice, he began to tell me a story. He did this so well, I sat and listened without interruption until he had finished.

'I think,' he said at the conclusion of his story, 'It's time we went back to our beds'

I had been so totally engrossed in his words, that I hadn't noticed the time passing by. As I looked up, I became aware that it was much brighter in the ward and agreed with my friend, it was time to leave our cosy 'den'.

'When will I see you again?' I asked him as we scrambled from behind the tree.

'Tonight,' he answered, 'Now quickly, get back to your bed!'

"I began to tip-toe back to bed and turning around at one point, I saw that I was alone. Believing my friend had returned to his own ward, I continued to my bed, all the while marvelling at how quietly he had slipped away. I reached my bed without being noticed by the nurse and immediately fell into a deep sleep.

"When I awoke once more it was daylight and a laughing nurse was standing by my bed.

'Well sleepy-head, I see those nightmares didn't

keep you awake after all,' she leaned forward and ruffled my hair and I smiled back at her. 'That makes a nice change,' she said on seeing my smile.

"With that she carried on down the ward, leaving me to my own thoughts. I felt considerably better that morning and I kept on thinking of my friend and our magical place behind the tree. I realised I did not know his name and I told myself I would ask him that night. That day was the best I had spent on the ward and when my Mother and sister called to see me, they were happy at my improvement.

"I tried to stay awake when finally night fell and we children were supposed to be getting our rest, but try as I might I just couldn't keep my eyes open. Somewhere, deep in sleep, I heard someone calling my name and awoke to find the boy sitting once more by my bed. Placing a finger on his lips to warn me to be quiet, he beckoned me to follow him. I was not reluctant and within moments we were 'tucked-up' behind the tree again. Once more he kept me entranced with a Christmas story, a story full of hope and happiness, magic and wonder. All too soon, it seemed, the morning arrived and we had to return to our beds. It was only on reaching mine, that I was dismayed to find, I had neglected once more, to find out his name.

"That morning I felt good again and the Doctor's were very happy with my noticeable improvement. I was told that if I carried on like this, I would be home for Christmas day! I was overjoyed with this news and could hardly wait to tell my friend. I had the opportunity to tell him that night as we hid in our usual spot. I also spoke for the first time about my Father and the troubles of our family. He was very sympathetic and understanding but he also said many things that filled me with hope, though I was not certain how he managed to do it. The night ended and amazingly I still had not leaned his name!

"I had noticed, the night before, that my friend was looking paler and thinner and when I met him yet again, his decline was all the more noticeable. I asked him about his illness but he told me not to worry. We spoke for hours that night, though for once it was I who was the cheerful and lively one. When the night was finally over, I returned as always, quietly to my bed. This time instead of disappearing to his own ward, the boy accompanied me and when I was settled beneath the covers, sat in the chair next to me. I was only a little surprised at this, for by this time, I was quite used to my friend's amazing ability to go unnoticed. Leaning close to me, he began to speak,

'Thomas, I think you will be going home very soon and so I came to say goodbye.'

"I was taken aback by this unexpected comment and my emotions were very mixed. The prospect of going home for Christmas was now, with thanks to him, something I longed for. Yet the thought of saying goodbye to my friend, who looked as though home was a long way off, was hard to bear.

'But what about you?' I asked, feeling a lump form in my throat. 'You'll be going home soon as well? I will see you again?'

'Yes,' he smiled, 'I will be going soon and I know I will see you again, although it might not be for a very long time. Now I really must go, goodbye Thomas, have a very happy Christmas, try never to forget how special Christmas is!'

I started to say my own goodbye, feeling very sad, when like a thunder-bolt it hit me. I still didn't know his name!

'Your name,' I gasped, 'You've never told me your name, I kept meaning to ask but somehow I always forgot to!'

He stood up and looked at me in such a strange way, that for a moment I was scared, then he smiled and I felt safe and warm again.

'My name is Robert,' and smiling down at me from what now seemed a great height he said, 'Now goodbye one last time… little brother'

"With these final words, he turned and walked quickly from the ward, leaving me stunned and shaking. His final words echoed in my head as I tried to comprehend the meaning of it all. For Robert was the name of my brother, my brother who had died a year before I was born.

"In the morning when I awakened, I was greeted by the sight of my Mother and sister. To my immense joy they told me they had come to take me home. The rest of the morning was spent saying goodbye and thank you, to all who had taken care of me and in the business of returning home, I had not forgotten what had transpired that night. However, I did ask one nurse, whom I particularly liked, about the other children's ward. She simply laughed when I asked her and informed me that there was only one ward.

"Christmas was wonderful that year. We may not have had some of the things of the past but we were so happy to have each other. Late on Christmas Day, when we were filled to the brim with good things and sitting contented before a blazing fire, I asked my Mother about my brother. She was surprised at my inquiry, for I had seldom asked of him before but she was not reluctant to talk about him. I heard of how a mysterious, childhood illness had carried him off, when he was the age I now was, but more important to me, she told of how special and happy a child he had been. Like most families, we kept an album of family photographs, of which I had paid little heed until now. Returning from her bedroom, where it was kept for safekeeping, my Mother placed the album before my sister and I.

"With giggling enthusiasm, my sister began to turn the pages, while I, with a feeling of expectation growing in me, looked on. At last she turned to a page that made my breath catch in my throat. In the rambling garden of our old house, there stood a tree. On this tree, Father had tied a rope to make a swing. I had spent many happy hours on this swing and it had distressed me greatly to leave it behind. The photo showed this tree and this swing but more importantly, it showed the happy, smiling face of my brother, Robert. It was a face I knew very well. It was the face of a boy who had taught me all about Christmas."

Chapter 4

The Carriage

Thomas, in a hushed voice, looked to Gabe and spoke again.

"I never, ever, forgot that particular Christmas and I always tried to keep it in my heart, as I knew Robert wanted, but these last few years have been so very hard. I just gave up hope but you knew all of this didn't you? How did you know? Just who are you anyway?"

Gabe addressed him, an answer that was also for Anne and Iain.

"Tell me, how do you feel? Are you angry, are you afraid?"

There was silence for a few moments and then

Thomas laughed. It was a deep and pleasant sound, which brought smiles to the faces of his three companions.

"I don't know why," Thomas said, trying and failing to suppress his laughter, "But I feel wonderful, better than I have felt for years in fact, I don't know what it is you have done Gabe," and here his voice was charged with sincerity. "But I thank you from the bottom of my heart."

Anne and Iain immediately expressed similar feelings of joy and gratitude and Gabe, his face one vast smile, thanked them for their kind words. A companionable silence fell on the carriage after these words, as though all were waiting for something to happen. The three travellers had been touched by an experience they did not understand and though undoubtedly, they had many questions they wished to ask, for some reason, they felt unable to do so.

Gabe finally broke this reverie, as turning to his companions he said, "Would you like it, if I told a story?"

As one, Anne, Iain and Thomas, turned to Gabe,

they did not answer him with words, for their looks were eloquent enough.

"This is a tale of long ago…" Gabe began…

Voyage

"Long ago, when ships with sails, still crossed the Seven Seas, there were three old sailors. They had spent all of their lives, from early youth onwards, serving before the mast. Now, at the end of their service, they were each making one last voyage together.

It is strange to relate, even though they had all served for so many years across the vast oceans, they had never served together. In actual fact, they had never met before and were complete strangers to one and other. There may have been many occasions when their paths might have crossed but never did. Perhaps one was sailing into port, just as another was leaving. Perhaps one was drinking rum in a smoky grog-shop, whilst another was having his sweethearts name tattooed on his chest. Whatever the reason, fate had kept them apart until now.

"It was not too long after the voyage had started, that the three old sailors, became acquainted with each other. Between them, there was a vast store of experience and knowledge and recognising this in each other, they soon became firm friends. The Captain of the ship, (a mere youth of fifty to them!) knew good men when he saw them and was therefore extremely happy to have the three old sailors with him. They, in their place, felt they were a cut above the rest of the crew and for the most part kept to their own company. Life had been hard on them, each had suffered pain and loss and each bore the scars of the hard and rugged lives they had led. One was minus an arm, the second, his leg and the third an eye. Perhaps these injuries also helped to draw them closer to each other. When they were not on duty, which wasn't very often, they shared a cabin and here they would eat, drink and more importantly, talk together. They spoke of days long past, when in their prime, they had roamed the world, bold and reckless and careless of the future. They spoke of their experiences at sea, of storms, gales, shipwrecks, treacherous seas and bone-chilling cold. Of verdant islands, exotic foods, azure skies and flying-fish. They spoke of Christmas, it being that time of year, of joy and thanksgiving, of family and friends, of home, warmth and comfort, the laughter of children and a partners loving hand. These especially were on their minds and in their hearts, for these had not been part of the life they had led for a long, long time.

"They talked also, of this, their last voyage and what they would do afterwards. Perhaps it is not so surprising, that they all had similar plans. They envisioned a small cottage close to the sea, where each day they could walk along the shore. With a pocket telescope and a pipe of good tobacco, they could watch the passing of ships, to their hearts content. In the evening, with all rude weathers safe outside, they could roast their toes before a roaring fire, a solid meal in their bellies and a good jug of ale at hand.

"The more they spoke of these matters, of their dreams and wishes, the more real they became.

Before too long, it was decided mutually, that three such good ship-mates, could billet together happily and be good company to each other, in the long days and nights that would follow. This decision filled each of them with happiness and they began to look forward to the end of the voyage with great anticipation.

"Whilst the three companions were busy with their dreams and happy in their future plans, they did not take too much note of the rest of the crew. If they had, they would have noted how unhappy they were. Sailors in those long gone days were, as a rule, superstitious. In the vast oceans of this world there are many inexplicable things. Things, that for those who see them, are the stuff, sometimes of dream and sometimes of nightmare. To behold such things, can leave one, feeling small and insignificant and in dire need of good-fortune and good-luck.

"The voyage, which had started so well, suffered a series of mishaps, each of which added to the growing unease of the crew. The first of these mishaps, was the discovery that a third of the water, contained in huge barrels, was tainted and undrinkable. There was still sufficient to last the voyage but only if it were rationed out carefully. The weather also played an important part in the feelings of unrest. This was not because it was bad but in fact the reverse. They had expected, at that time of the year and in that particular sea, high winds and a fast passage. Instead, after the first couple of days, the winds had dropped till barely a whisper stirred the canvas and consequently movement was slow.

"Added to this were bouts of uncalled for anger and worse still unnecessary actions, some of which were violent. The final piece of bad luck, which confirmed to some that the voyage was doomed, was the death of the ship's cat!

"To some, this may seem an minor upset, not worthy of such a fuss but not so the crew. The cat, a tangle-haired, battle-scarred, old tom, had been a great favourite of the crew. This was not only because of his ability as a rat-catcher but also because of his genial temperament. His sudden and inexplicable demise came as a terrible shock and even the most level-headed of the crew felt an ill omen had overtaken them. This sense of gathering doom began to affect work on board the ship. Men became sloppy and careless and an atmosphere of futility pervaded almost the whole ship.

"It may have been because of this atmosphere, that things turned out as they did. Or perhaps it was just one of those things, one more piece of bad luck, or just blind fate, no one will ever know. One morning, in the early hours, a tremendous storm blew up. It caught everyone by surprise, even the Captain and the three old sailors. The man who was on watch, normally a very conscientious and hard working sailor, had fallen asleep at his post. This had never happened to him before but he had not slept for the last three nights. He was a superstitious man and had been badly effected by the mood aboard the ship.

"It was truly a terrible storm, sea and sky were equally black and inseparable to the eye. Waves, dwarfing the ship, shot heaven-wards before crashing with a monstrous roar onto the fragile ship below. The best crew in the world, at the height of their strength and confident of their ability, may just have survived the awful onslaught. Unfortunately this crew, already suffering under a cloud, were not up to the task. Each sailor acquitted themselves bravely but it was all for naught. One gigantic wave, a wave that made the ones before it look insignificant, hovered, horribly tantalising, above them. Then with one last mighty thunder-clap of sound, fell onto the ship and drove her deep below the sea. It was the end for the brave little ship, her back broke in two and the relentless, unforgiving, sea swallowed her.

"As fate would have it, the three old sailors were cast into the sea almost together. They had been above deck when she went down and had been thrown, like rag-dolls, into the boiling trough of the sea. The water was as black as ink and chilled them, within moments, to the bone. Clinging desperately to a broken beam and each other, they made valiant and desperate efforts to stay afloat. Time passed with incredible slowness, as the three friends became weaker and weaker. They each knew, their lives were hanging by a slender thread and as one they offered up a silent prayer.

"Dawn broke and with it brought new hope. The seas, which had pounded and pulled at them relentlessly, began to subside as the storm finally blew itself out. As the light grew, the three men found themselves floating, in the vast and empty ocean. There were no signs of their ship or their former comrades and they sadly feared the worst. Their spirits, which had revived slightly with dawn's arrival, wavered once again. They knew their chances of survival were almost non-existent. For if hunger, thirst or the cold did not get them, surely the sharks would. It was at this precise moment, when all hope had fled, that they saw, coming towards them, a small craft. They could not believe their luck and began to shout and call with all their might. As the craft drew closer, they observed it was being rowed, with deep, strong strokes, by a single, tall man.

"With remarkable precision the boat heaved to directly in front of them and its occupant lent over the side. They found themselves looking into a smiling face and being offered a welcome, helping hand. With

amazing strength, the man pulled the three ship-
wrecked sailors into his boat and dipping his oars
once more into the sea, set off at a steady pace. The
three men heartily thanked him and were about to ask
him several questions, when he forestalled them. He
invited the men to open a large trunk that lay in the
bottom of his boat and this they did. Inside to their
utter astonishment, were three sets of dry clothes and
an ample supply of food and drink for three people.
The man told them, to feel free to change their clothes
and to eat and drink their fill. This was said in such a
kindly manner, that the three forgot about their
questions and did as they were bid.

"As they ate and drank the man told them the
most wonderful news. Their friends and former
colleagues had all been rescued, not a single soul had
been lost! This was good news almost beyond belief
but the three men did not doubt the stranger's word
for one second.

"When they were warmed, dried and full of good
food and drink they settled with contented sighs in the
bottom of the boat. Though they were filled with

burning questions, who had rescued their friends? Where had he come from in this vast sea? Who was he? They each felt somehow it was wrong to ask. Similarly, they were also without any feelings of fear or suspicion, instead they each felt an overwhelming sense of peace. A companionable silence fell on the boat, as she moved at a steady pace towards her unknown destination.

"This silence was finally broken, when one old sailor began to sing. It was an ancient song, but familiar to all. A song of Christmas, a song of hope and love. A score of voices singing it, may have shaken the dust from many a church eaves, a single voice might have brought a tear to an eye. Deep and rough, yet rich and true, the sailor's voice drifted across the sea. All at once, his friends and the stranger joined him in song and their voices carried to the sky.

As the final note faded across the waves, each man shook hands and bade his fellows a Happy Christmas.

"The stranger, setting aside his oars, turned to the three old men with a smile.

'Look, you are nearly home,' and he pointed beyond them.

"As one man, the three old companions looked in the direction of the pointing hand and a feeling of awe and wonder struck them silent. In the near distance was a soft hump of land, green and fertile. This, until the stranger had spoken, had been completely invisible to them. On its long golden shore there stood a cabin with an open door. A warm and welcoming light shone forth from this door and inside vague shadows moved. What was that scent that made their noses tingle? Was it fresh bread, sweet and soft? Was it newly-cut flowers or bright, clean sheets? What were those sounds they heard, carried on the gentle breeze? Were they the sounds of children playing, or the laughter of friends? Or was it possible, could it be, was it the voice of a dear one calling to them?

"The friends turned to the stranger, with questions finally coming to their lips, only to find he was no longer sitting in the boat! He had completely vanished and they could find no trace of him.

'Perhaps we shouldn't ask any questions,' the

sailor who had started the song, said to his companions. 'Our strange friend has brought us to a place, we have always longed to be, shall we just go there and not ask why or how?'

"His friends nodded silently in agreement, as if they too realised, that now was not the time for questions. They looked at each other, each with the knowledge that all they had known was now over but they were not afraid or sad. The boat of its own volition, carried them to land and the three climbed out on to that golden shore. Smiling they began to walk towards the cabin, to the open door, to the warmth and welcome of a place called Home."

Chapter 5

The carriage

Thomas was the first to speak, as Gabe's story came to an end, his voice cracked with emotion.

"Gabe, please tell us who you are?" he pleaded, "Where are we really going? This story of the three sailors it means something doesn't it? Are they... are they meant to be us?"

Anne and Iain, both said similar words, though in truth, they and Thomas, in their hearts, already knew the answers.

"Yes," he answered them, his voice filled with compassion, "The three sailors could in fact be you, for they were searching for something, that they had denied themselves for so many years, and is that not true of yourselves? Each of you has been blighted by tragedy or loss, that has stolen your hopes and your dreams. The death of parents, (here he looked to Iain) a marriage devoid of love, (here he looked to Anne) and high ambitions turned to avarice (finally he looked to Thomas). These have made you forget the wonders you have encountered in your lives, made you lose the spirit that dwells within you. I have come here to remind you and to prepare you, for the continuation of your journey."

The train at this point, began to slow down and through the windows that had been covered in frost and snow, a golden light began to shine. A golden light that shimmered and danced, burnishing each face with gentle hue.

"We have arrived," Gabe motioned to the three travellers, "It is time for us to alight."

"Before we leave," Thomas asked, who once so reluctant to speak, had now become the spokesman for all three, "You must tell us, we must know. Are we dead?"

"Would it be true to say," Gabe kindly answered,

"That to be dead, is to be devoid of all feeling, all hope, all aspirations, all love? Is this how you feel now?"

The travellers indicated it was not.

"My dear friends," Gabe continued, "You have simply ended one journey and a new one is about to begin. Come with me now, let me show you, let me be your guide and friend."

Holding hands, the companions stepped down from the train into the golden light. As feelings of profound joy and reverence fell over them, a voice filled with compassion and love spoke to them.

"Welcome home," said Gabriel.